Dear mouse friends,
Welcome to the world of

Geronimo Stilton

THE RODENT'S GAZETTE
EDITORIAL STAFF

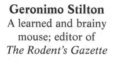

Geronimo Stilton
A learned and brainy
mouse; editor of
The Rodent's Gazette

Thea Stilton
Geronimo's sister and
special correspondent at
The Rodent's Gazette

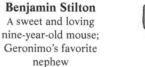

Trap Stilton
An awful joker;
Geronimo's cousin and
owner of the store
Cheap Junk for Less

Benjamin Stilton
A sweet and loving
nine-year-old mouse;
Geronimo's favorite
nephew

Geronimo Stilton

THE MOUSE ISLAND MARATHON

Scholastic Inc.

New York   Toronto   London   Auckland   Sydney
Mexico City   New Delhi   Hong Kong   Buenos Aires

No part of this publication may be reproduced in any form or by any means, electronic, mechanical, photocopying, recording, or otherwise, without written permission of the publisher. For information regarding permission, write to Scholastic Inc., Attention Permissions Department, 557 Broadway, New York, NY 10012.

ISBN 13: 978-0-439-84121-4
ISBN 10: 0-439-84121-6

Published by Scholastic Inc.
SCHOLASTIC and associated logos are trademarks and/or registered trademarks of Scholastic Inc.

Stilton is the name of a famous English cheese. It is a registered trademark of the Stilton Cheese Makers' Association. For more information, go to www.stiltoncheese.com.

Text by Geronimo Stilton
Original title: *La maratona più pazza del mondo!*
Cover by Giuseppe Ferrario
Illustrations by Valeria Turati
Graphics by Merenguita Gingermouse

Special thanks to Kathryn Cristaldi
Interior design by Kay Petronio

12 11 10 9 8 7 6 5   8 9 10 11 12/0

Printed in the U.S.A.
First printing, June 2007

HOLEY CHEESE . . .

It was a beautiful summer morning. The sun was shining like a round ball of cheddar in the sky. *What a great day,* I thought as I headed off for work.

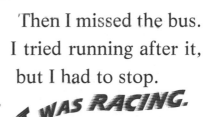

Then I missed the bus. I tried running after it, but I had to stop. **MY HEART WAS RACING.** My whiskers were sweating. And I could barely **breathe**!

Holey cheese, I was out of shape!

Eventually, I made it to the office. Oops, I almost forgot to introduce myself. My name is Stilton,

Geronimo Stilton. I am the publisher of *The Rodent's Gazette,* the most famouse newspaper on Mouse Island.

Anyway, I got to the office just as my sister **ROARED** through the lobby. Yes, I mean roared. She likes to ride her motorcycle indoors!

"Wow, big brother, I just heard the news. When did you turn into such a **SPORTSMOUSE?**" she chattered, grinning.

I shook my head. I definitely wasn't a **SPORTSMOUSE**. I could barely chew a

cheese stick and walk at the same time.

Just then, my cousin Trap strolled in. "Hey, Germeister. How's the training going? Who would have thought a wimpy rodent like you would become such a **SPORTSMOUSE**?" he snickered.

A minute later, my nephew Benjamin appeared. He tugged at my sleeve.

"Uncle Geronimo, what are you doing in the office? A **SPORTSMOUSE** like you should be out running in the park. After all, you're in training," he *squeaked*.

I twisted my tail up in a knot. Had my whole family gone **crazy**? The last time I went for a stroll in the park, I tripped over a pinecone and twisted my ankle. I was on crutches for three weeks!

"Would someone please tell me what you are all squeaking about?" I shouted, plopping down behind my desk.

Before they could answer, a rodent strode into my office. He wore bicycle shorts, sunglasses and a whistle. I would know that mouse anywhere. It was my friend **Champ Strongpaws**.

CHAMP STRONGPAWS

First Name: Champ

Last Name: Strongpaws

Background info: An all-around star athlete. He's into the latest training trends. He works for a sports radio station, and loves to get lazy rodents up and running.

Sports: He does all kinds of endurance sports like cycling, running, and swimming. And he loves marathons!

His advice: Eat right, sleep right, and keep those paws pumping.

What he believes in: Exercise!

His passion: Exploring new countries and getting to experience other cultures.

His slogan: "Sports can make the world a better place!"

His claim to fame: He built a super-fast bicycle that can seat five mice.

His dream: To explore the ten most beautiful countries in the world in ten days, with ten different bicycles.

A MARATHON?

Champ slapped me on the back. I checked for broken bones. Did I mention that Champ is a super-muscular mouse?

"Oops," he snickered. "Guess I don't know my own strength. Speaking of strength, we'll need to build up those puny muscles of yours, Mr. G. After all, I've entered you in THE MOUSE ISLAND MARATHON!"

Marathon? I blinked. I could never run a marathon. I couldn't even chew cheese and wiggle my ears at the same time.

But before I could protest, the door to my office burst open. The entire staff of *The Rodent's Gazette* marched inside.

"Congratulations, Geronimo! You're going to be a marathon mouse!"

They **lifted** me up into the air and carried me out of the room. The outer office had been decorated with tons of balloons and colorful streamers, and there were lots of snacks!

I was just about to stuff my snout with a few yummy doughnuts when **Champ** slapped them out of my paw.

"**NONE OF THAT,** Mr. G," he ordered. "You can't run a marathon unless you eat healthy foods."

Then he offered me a carrot stick.

Oh, why did Champ pick *me* to do something athletic? "So, um, how long is this marathon race thing?" I muttered.

Champ grinned. "It's nothing, Mr. G. Just a mere twenty-six point two miles."

I almost choked on my carrot. "Twenty-six miles?!! **Twenty-six miles?!!**"

I squeaked. "What kind of a race is twenty-six miles long? **THAT'S CRAZY!**"

Champ's grin grew even wider. "That's right, Mr. G. And they call the Mouse Island Marathon the craziest marathon *ever*!"

I pictured myself running. But not in the race — away from Champ Strongpaws! Far, far away where no one would ever find me. Then I fainted.

Kreamy O'Cheddar, my editor in chief, had to revive me with her Parmesan cheese-scented smelling salts.

ONE TWO, ONE TWO, ONE TWO . . .

The next morning, I was snoring away peacefully in my bed when the doorbell rang. Ding-dong! Ding-dong! I opened one bleary eye. Who would be ringing my doorbell at such an unmousely hour?

I shuffled to the front door in a daze. **Champ** was standing on my WELCOME RAT mat. "Wakey-wakey, Mr. G! Training begins today!" he screeched.

I thought I must be having a nightmare. But then Champ began to sing. Loudly.

"The sun is up, so come on, lazy mousey. Come on out of your cozy housey!"

I put my paws over my ears, hoping **Champ** would take the hint. Unfortunately,

Champ didn't seem to care.

He dragged me out onto my front stoop in my pajamas. "Come on, Mr. G., it's time for your morning run." I was *mortified*. What if someone saw me?

Champ's squeak interrupted my thoughts. "One two, one two, **keep those knees up**!" he yelled. He ran alongside of me, checking his stopwatch every few seconds.

I felt sick. My muscles were aching. My head was pounding. Even my fur hurt.

Champ made me run around the block thirty times. Finally, I collapsed outside the local flower shop. Green Paws, the florist, came running out.

Champ dragged me out.... He made me run around the block.... I felt sick....

"Mr. Stilton, are you feeling OK?" he asked worriedly. "You look a little green around the leaves, as we say in the flower business."

I wanted to tell him I was not OK. Far from it. But I was so exhausted, I could hardly breathe. Sweat dripped down my fur like water from a leaky shower faucet.

Two minutes later, I was hit with another shower.

Champ dumped a whole vase of cold

He dumped cold water on my head.

I passed out!

water on my head.

"**Aaah!**" I yelled.

Champ looked satisfied. "Now, let's see here, for the rest of the week, your training program will include a five-mile run, three hundred laps in the pool, and **two hours of weightlifting**. That'll separate the strong mice from the weak, right, Mr. G?" he chuckled.

I wanted to reply, but I was too busy bawling my eyes out.

Oh, how did I get myself into such a mess?

YOUR TURN, GERONIMO!

The next morning, **Champ** took me to Fastfur Fields, a sports complex for serious athletes. I, Geronimo Stilton, am not a serious athlete.

In the afternoon, **Champ** took me to play soccer with some of his friends. I got hit in the head with the ball twenty-five times!

Then we were off to Crunchers, New Mouse City's most exclusive gym. **Champ** made me lift weights. I fainted.

Finally, Champ took me to a huge indoor swimming pool. I was doing great until he took my rubber ducky float away.

The serious sportsmice at Fastfur Fields!

Then Champ made me jump off
the highdive and swim laps!

24/7

Days went by. Every morning was the same. **Champ** woke me up at 6 A.M. to go running. I started to go to bed in my sweatsuit just so I could sleep for a few extra minutes. Did I mention I'm not a morning mouse?

But Champ wouldn't let up. He made me run the same route every day. I ran all over the streets of New Mouse City. I finished at the New Mouse City Public Library. Have you ever been there? You have to climb up sixty-seven steps to even get to the front door.

I didn't **climb**. I **CRAWLED**.

Champ ran behind me, shouting advice. *"Don't give up! Don't give in!* Don't give a strange rodent your phone number. **It's just not safe,**" he babbled.

My family loved to watch me run. Trap waited for me by his kitchen window. He put a piece of cheese on a fishing line and dangled it above my head. "Come and get it, Gerry Berry!" he taunted.

Thea chased after me on her motorcycle. "Better move your tail, little brother, or **I'll run you over!**" she teased.

Then there was Benjamin. Every day he met me at his school bus stop with a delicious yogurt shake. "This is for you, Uncle. You're doing great!" he cheered.

Thank goodness for my dear sweet nephew.

After a few weeks, something amazing happened. I didn't huff and puff when I ran anymore. I didn't feel faint. I didn't cry uncontrollably when I got out of bed in the morning. Well, except for the day I tripped over my catfur rug and broke my pawnail.

Yes, I, Geronimo Stilton, was starting to feel like maybe **I wasn't such a sports failure after all.**

Of course, working out with Champ wasn't easy. He was in my snout 24/7. *He told me when to run. When to rest. And even what to eat!* **Champ** had thrown out all of the fattening food in my refrigerator, even my Cheesy Chews. I was heartbroken. Still, I had to admit I was getting **STRONGER**. I had more energy. After three weeks, I even climbed up the steps to the library without stopping!

I surprised everyone, especially myself. **I DESERVED A REWARD!** Now if only I could find those Cheesy Chews . . .

I even climbed the steps to the library without stopping!

I WANT TO GO HOOOOME!

Months passed, and Champ made me train harder every day. Soon it was time to set off for the marathon.

The race was going to take place in the city of Nibbles. Nibbles is on the opposite side of Mouse Island, overlooking Stray Cat Harbor.

The plane ride took **twenty million hours**. Well, OK, maybe not twenty million, but it was super-long.

I tried to take a nap, but **Champ** wanted to give me advice about the *marathon*. "Now listen up, Mr. G. Whatever you do, don't worry about the twenty-six long, exhausting, painful, backbreaking miles ahead of you. Don't worry if you're moving slower than a

snail with arthritis. Don't worry if you feel weaker than an ANT with a broken leg. Don't worry if you're more tired than a hibernating SLOTH. Just concentrate on finishing the race," he squeaked.

Oh, why had I agreed to enter this crazy race? I wasn't an athlete. I was a newspaper mouse.

"I want to go home!" I sobbed.

But **Champm** just grinned. "Don't be ridiculous, Mr. G. I didn't spend all that time training you for nothing. *You'll do great.*"

To take my mind off things, I decided to read the paper. Bad idea. Staring up at me from the front page was a photo of a huge, **terrifying** cat. *Felinius ferociousmus,* otherwise known as Fifi the cat, was an

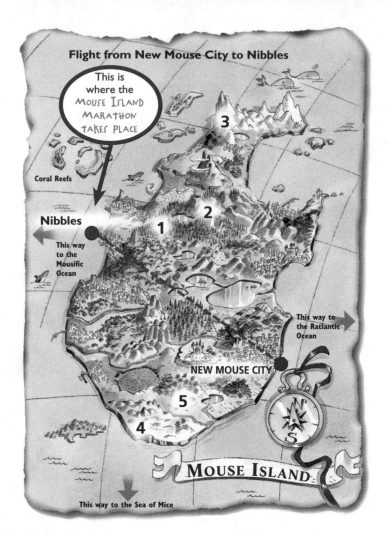

Flight from New Mouse City to Nibbles

This is where the MOUSE ISLAND MARATHON TAKES PLACE

Coral Reefs

Nibbles

This way to the Mousific Ocean

This way to the Ratlantic Ocean

NEW MOUSE CITY

MOUSE ISLAND

This way to the Sea of Mice

1. **Brimstone Lake**
2. **Roastedrat Volcano**
3. **Frozen Fur Park**
4. **Mousehara Desert**
5. **Rio Mosquito**

The city of Nibbles is on the westernmost tip of Mouse Island. It overlooks the Rattenburg River and Stray Cat Harbor, famous for its huge (and very hungry) sharks.

Nibbles is known for its very strange climate, which is constantly changing. When the north wind blows the temperatures are icy, and when the south wind blows it's like living in an oven!

• THE CITY OF NIBBLES •

ROUTE OF THE MOUSE ISLAND MARATHON

extremely rare species. She had escaped from the Natural Science Mouseum of Nibbles, where scientists had been studying her. Now the whole city of Nibbles was running from Fifi.

I stared at the picture of the horrifying wild cat. Then I noticed my fellow passengers. They looked as **WILD** as Fifi. And they were all headed to the marathon, too.

How did I know they were marathon runners? That's easy:

1. They were *all* wearing expensive track suits.
2. They *all* took turns racing one another

UP AND DOWN the aisles.

3. They *all* drank from big water bottles.

4. They *all* ate energy bars.

5. They *all* read fitness magazines.

6. They *all* had big muscles.

7. They *all* looked like they'd be finished with the race before I even crossed the **STARTING LINE**!

I sank down in my seat. Oh, when would this nightmare be over?

Finally, it was time for lunch. At last, something to celebrate! I licked my whiskers.

Right then, the flight attendant passed me

a plate. I almost cried out loud. Three lettuce leaves, two raw carrots, and a boiled turnip stared back at me.

I pulled the attendant aside. "Um, excuse me, madam. Is there any way you could get me something a little less healthy? Like a big slab of cheddar lasagna?" I whispered.

The flight attendant smiled. But next to me, Champ frowned. Rats!

"Mr. G, I'm very disappointed in you," he scolded. "You know you're in training. In fact, madam, can you please remove one of these lettuce leaves? My friend here is on a very strict diet."

I chewed my pawnail in dismay. Oh, if only it were a delicious piece of chocolate cake!

With a sigh, I picked up a carrot. I took a bite. It tasted like a piece of rubber. YUCK!

After the carrot, I needed to get rid of the rubber taste. I picked up my cup. It was filled with some kind of strange, lumpy brown liquid. I think it was one of those energy drinks. I took a sip. I gagged. This drink sure gave me energy. I felt like hurling my cup out the window!

I picked up a carrot.

I was so hungry, I decided there was only one thing left to do. I had to use my imagination. I pretended the carrot was a slice of cheese pizza and the energy drink was a yummy mozzarella milk shake. Quickly, I tried gulping them down together. It didn't work. All I tasted was rubber and a cross between sour pickles and curdled milk.

I picked up my cup.

I tried gulping them down together.

All I tasted was rubber and...curdled milk.

DIIIIIIIING
DIIIIIIIIIING!

At last, the plane landed in Nibbles.

I was exhausted. When we reached the hotel, I crawled straight into bed.

"Don't forget to set your alarm clock. The big race is tomorrow," **Champ** reminded me.

I sat up in bed. **Holey cheese!** I was so tired, I had forgotten all about the marathon. I started to worry. What if I tripped? What if I fainted?

I didn't shut my eyes until 6 A.M. Two minutes later, the alarm went off.

Diiiiiiiiiiing!

Diiiiiiiiiiiing!

I was a wreck.

When I got to the hotel lobby, I noticed something strange. A lot of the other runners had bags under their eyes, too.

Maybe I wasn't the only one who was nervous!

A mouse with pretty honey-colored fur tapped my shoulder.

"Is this your first marathon?" she asked. "Mine, too. I'm Honey Fur."

I smiled. Maybe this marathon business wasn't so bad after all.

"Um, yes, well, uh, my name is Stilton, *Geronimo Stilton* . . ." I began.

But I was interrupted by **Champ**. He stood on a platform near a huge open window. In one paw he held a microphone. In the other, he held a stack of notecards.

"Dear rodent friends, I'd like to welcome you all to THE MOUSE ISLAND MARATHON,"

THE MARATHON

The oldest long-distance running race became an Olympic sport at the world's first modern edition of the games in 1896.

The name marathon goes back to 490 b.c. when the Greek soldier Pheidippides ran from the battlefield of Marathon to Athens (24.85 miles) to announce victory over the Persians.

The length of the marathon was initially fixed according to the distance run by Pheidippides (24.85 miles), but following the 1908 London Olympics, the distance was changed to its present length: 26.2 miles. This corresponds to the distance between Windsor Castle (where the race began) and the White City stadium (where it ended).

Over the years, the marathon has been adopted as a major sporting event by several of the world's most important cities. The oldest annual marathon is the Boston Marathon, which has been around since 1897!

he squeaked, reading his speech off the cards. "For some of you, this is your first marathon, and I want to congratulate you on your courage. You will soon see that running a marathon is a truly *wonderful* experience."

Right then, a big **GUST** of wind blew in the window. It picked up Champ's cards and tossed them all over the room.

"My speech," Champ MUTTERED, looking lost. I decided to help Champ out. I grabbed the microphone from him.

"Um, well, hello, my name is Geronimo Stilton, and I'm very excited to be running my first marathon today," I **stammered**. "I've been training really hard for this race. I've even given up all of my favorite foods like triple deluxe cheddar burgers, and my dear aunt Ratilda's homemade cream cheese."

Before I knew it, I was drooling all over the microphone.

I looked around. The other runners were DROOLING, too. Champ glared at me. Uh-oh.

I didn't mean to cause a scene, making everyone remember the foods they'd given up. Still, could I help it if I just couldn't say no to CREAM CHEESE?

It Figures . . .

Before I knew it, it was time to start the race. Runners spilled out of the hotel. We were greeted by a rush of **frozen air**. It was snowing!

Luckily, I was prepared. I pulled a hat over my ears and wrapped a scarf around my snout. I stumbled blindly through the snow. A minute later, I walked smack into another runner. "Watch where you're going, Furball," the mouse muttered. His voice sounded familiar. It was **GLOOMY GUS VON CACKLEFUR!** He was the uncle of my strange friend, Creepella von Cacklefur. Gloomy Gus was just as weird as his niece. And he was always complaining about something.

"It figures we'd get stuck running in the

middle of a snowstorm, eh, Geronimo?" he grumbled. "The weather in Nibbles is the **WORST**. When the north wind blows, your fur turns to icicles. When the south wind blows, you can **FRY** an egg on your snout."

I listened politely as Gloomy Gus **MOANED** and **GROANED** about, well, everything. I shook my head in sympathy. What else could I do? There was no cheering up old Gloomy Gus. In fact, if you looked up the word **miserable** in the dictionary, you'd probably find his picture next to it.

KEEP YOUR PAWS ON THE GROUND!

The marathon's starting line was on a giant bridge. I could hardly believe the crowd. It was **huge**! There were young rodents, old rodents, and rodents of all different sizes, shapes, and colors. There were serious athletes and *cheese puffs*, like me.

Some athletes were blind and were paired with guides. Others were in special wheelchairs, which they moved using their paws.

What an *amazing sight*. For the first time, I started to relax. If rodents with disabilities could do a **marathon**, maybe

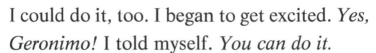

I could do it, too. I began to get excited. *Yes, Geronimo!* I told myself. *You can do it.*

Then, out of the corner of my eye, I spotted a beat-up old pickup truck. The rat who was driving it looked just like an **undertaker**. A sign on the back of the truck read, REST IN PIECES.

"Don't worry if you don't make it. I'll pick up your remains," the rat **snickered** through the window.

A **shiver** ran down my fur. Oh, who

was I kidding? I wasn't an athlete. I couldn't run a marathon. Even though it was freezing outside, I broke into a sweat. My head began to pound. MY PAWS SHOOK.

An OLD mouse patted me on the shoulder.

"Don't be nervous, Sonny. All you have to do is keep your paws on the ground and keep reaching for the stars," he advised. "My name is *Old Rat Rickety,* but you can call me Rickety for short. I've been running marathons for thirty-five years, and let me tell you, they never get boring. Yep, something tells me this one's going to be the **craziest** yet!"

I gulped. Old Rat Rickety was starting to

Old Rat Rickety

look a little crazy himself. His eyes gleamed. His whiskers whirled in the wind. Before he moved on, he whispered one last bit of advice in my ear.

"Just remember, Sonny," he squeaked. "Never give up. Never stop believing in yourself. And never get the prune cheese rolls at Stop and Squeak. They're awful!"

I was about to ask Rickety what he thought about the cherry cheese danish, when a mouse wearing an official-looking suit held up his paw.

Everyone on the bridge grew silent.

"All marathon runners line up, please!" the mouse squeaked into a megaphone.

Then he blew a horn so loud I nearly jumped right out of my fur. The marathon was starting!

ON YOUR MARK,
GET SET . . . GO!!!

"On your mark, get set . . . **GO!!!**" the official mouse yelled.

And we were off. I must admit, it was incredible. Thirty-two thousand rodents running all at once!

I took off along the bridge.

After a little while, we hit a sign that read MILE ONE. I was so proud of myself. So far, I didn't feel tired at all.

I guess all those torturous mornings with Champ had really **PAID OFF**.

On both sides of the road, the crowd cheered us along.

"**Bravo, bravo!**" an old mouse with white fur cried.

"You can do it!" his friend added.

"Yippee!" A baby mouselet clapped her paws.

Everyone wanted to see us run. I felt like a real **CELEBRITY**. I pushed my shoulders back and straightened my scarf, just in case anyone wanted to take my picture. You never know.

Some of the spectators carried signs. They said things like, "Keep up the pace!"

"You're the best!" and "**Shake a paw, Grandma Beady Eyes!**"

That last one gave me a tiny pang. I wished my family could have been there to cheer me on, too.

After three miles, I stopped at a water station. **Champ** always told me how **important** it is to drink liquids while you're exercising.

A smiling race assistant passed me a

plastic cup of water. Then he threw his paws around my neck. At first, I panicked. Was he trying to strangle me? Was he after my expensive cheddar-colored scarf?

Then the mouse squeaked in my ear, **"SURPRISE,** Uncle!" It was my nephew Benjamin. "I'm here to cheer you on. You're doing great!" he cried.

Did I mention I have the *sweetest* nephew in the world?

SNAP OUT OF IT!

After seeing Benjamin, I had new **energy**. I ran and ran.

I was actually feeling OK. But after thirteen miles, everything started to go downhill. No, I'm not talking about the road. I'm talking about yours truly. I felt awful!

My paws were **heavier** than two blocks of my grouchy grandma Onewhisker's fruit cheesecakes. My knees were **SHAKING**. And I had **SPRAINED** my tail.

I wanted to stop. I wanted to rest. I wanted to check in to the nearest day spa and get a two-hour massage.

Just then, the creepy rat with the **beat-up pickup truck** pulled alongside of me. He opened the door.

"Ready to give up? I'll take you away," he smirked.

I was so scared that I took off again, sobbing like a newborn mouselet.

"I can't do it! I can't do it!" I wailed.

"Snap out of it, little brother. Of course you can do it!"

A familiar voice called out.

I stopped crying and opened my eyes wide. Trap and Thea were standing right in front of me.

In a flash, Trap shoved a thick piece

of cheddar into my mouth. "The mouse in the cheese shop told me this cheddar has double the protein of your ordinary cheese. You'd better like it, Germeister. It cost me a bundle," he squeaked.

I gobbled down the cheese in one bite. It was **AMAZING**.

But I still wanted to quit.

"This marathon is too long for me . . ." I blubbered.

Thea rolled her eyes. "**OF COURSE** it's long," she snickered. "That's why it's called a marathon. Now stop whining and start running. You don't want to tell Champ he wasted his time with you, do you?"

I gulped. Thea was right. Champ would have a fit if I gave up now.

I kept on running. Oh, my **aching** paws!

ROASTED MOUSE!

After twenty miles, the south wind started blowing. It came from the **Mousehara Desert**. Now it was hot, hot, hot!

I took off my hat, scarf, and tracksuit. **IT WAS BOILING!** My whiskers were dripping with sweat.

At that moment, the sky turned a funny yellow color. Before I could say cheese niblets, there was a tremendous blast of wind. A second later, I couldn't see a thing! I was covered from head to paw with sand. It was a **sandstorm**!

"Everyone get down!" another runner yelled. We crouched down together behind a wall. It sheltered us from the wind and sand. We covered our snouts with handkerchiefs,

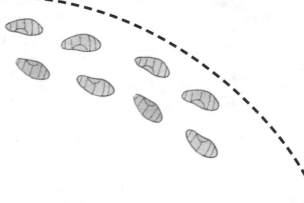

so that the sand couldn't get in our mouths and noses.

A car motor rumbled in the distance. I just knew it was that creepy rat in the pickup truck. He couldn't wait for someone to drop.

I shivered. I hoped it wouldn't be me.

I decided to pass the time by humming nursery rhymes. Everyone joined in. We were just finishing the second chorus of "Pop Goes the Gerbil," when the storm ended.

I wiped off my glasses, said good-bye to the other runners, and took off.

Bzzzz . . . Bzzzzz . . . Bzzzzzzz!

I had only gone a little farther when I heard a strange buzzing noise.

The buzzing got louder and louder.

All of a sudden, a black cloud fell over me. It was a giant swarm of bloodthirsty mosquitoes!

The mosquitoes made a feast of my fur. I felt like the strawberry cheesecake at my nephew's birthday party. Every bug wanted a piece of **me**!

I tried slapping them away, but it was no use. They just kept coming back for more. I

55

was being **eaten alive**! Headlines flashed before my eyes: MOUSE-HUNGRY MOSQUITOES MAKE A MEAL OUT OF PUBLISHER! GERONIMO STILTON: ALL CHEWED UP AND NOWHERE TO GO!

Finally, after I ran and ran, the **buzzing** stopped. I opened one eye. The cloud of black **mosquitoes** swirled off into the sky.

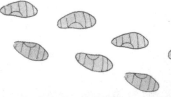

WET UP TO THE WHISKERS!

I was so happy to be away from the sand and the mosquitoes. For a moment, I almost forgot that I was running in a crazy marathon. I felt the warm sun on my fur. I listened to the birds singing in the trees. *Ah, what a beautiful day,* I thought.

Then I noticed a pretty little pond off to the side of the road. It looked so calm and peaceful. I scampered over and dipped one sore paw into the water. The cold water felt fabumouse! I leaned over to splash my snout. Big mistake.

SPLASH! I fell headfirst into the pond. I was wet up to my whiskers! **Green** scum from the bottom of the pond stuck to my fur as I pulled myself out of the water.

Just then, the rat in the pickup truck pulled up. **"You smell worse than the mice at the morgue,"** he snickered. **"Ready to call it quits? I'm sure they'd love to meet you."**

I shivered.

Pond scum flew in all directions.

Smack! Some of it hit the driver right in the snout. He took off with a scowl.

That'll teach him, I giggled to myself.

A SCHOOL IN FLAMES

I started running again. My paws **POUNDED** the pavement. Just as I turned the corner, it smelled like something was burning. In the distance, I could see a school building sitting on a hill.

FLAMES shot from the roof!

I signaled to some of the other runners. "Quick, they need our help!" I squeaked.

WE GOT THERE IN THE NICK OF TIME. Crying mouselets **STUMBLED OUT** of the exits, while their teachers tried to keep them calm.

One mouselet was missing.

I didn't stop. I just ran inside. Burning embers were falling everywhere. The roof started to cave in.

I was scared out of my fur. But what could I do? I had to find that mouselet.

Finally, I found the terrified mouse in the school's music room. He was hiding under the piano. I scooped him up and carried him outside to safety.

Everyone clapped and cheered when we emerged safely outside. I felt like a big cheese.

I took off on the race again. But this time, I had a huge smile on my snout.

EARTHQUAKE!

I was still smiling as I scampered by a grassy field. But before long, I noticed something **ODD**. The grass seemed to be rising.

I squinted. What was going on? Was I dreaming? Was I going blind? Was I headed for the Mad Mouse Center?

Just then, the earth began to shake beneath my paws. *Now* I knew what was going on. I had read about it in *The City of Nibbles Guidebook*. Every ten years or so, the place got hit by an earthquake.

Rat-munching rattlesnakes!

I felt faint with fear. I took off my glasses so I could cry freely. "*I want my mommy!*" I squeaked. Then I noticed a blurry figure to one side of me. I squinted. It was Honey Fur, the pretty rodent I had met at the beginning of the race. Oh, why did I always have to act like such a 'fraidy mouse?

Just then, we heard someone shouting. A gaping chasm had opened up in the middle of the road. One of the runners was about to **FALL** to the bottom.

I had an idea. Quickly, I gathered everyone's running jackets. I tied them together to form a rope. Then, we pulled the runner to safety.

Honey Fur patted my paw. "Great idea," she whispered.

I grinned. Score one for the 'fraidy mouse!

HOLD ON TIGHT!

I was so proud of myself. I felt a sudden burst of energy. I felt strong. I felt focused. I felt . . . WET? I looked down. Holey cheesecake! I was so busy rescuing the other runner, I hadn't heard the sound of rushing water.

"Look out! The Rattenburg River has burst its banks!" a mouse called.

All of the marathoners began to panic.

Crashing waves suddenly surrounded us. I was **TERRIFIED**. I grabbed the paw of the mouse next to me. That gave me an idea.

"Hold on tight to each other. If we do that, maybe we won't be swept away!" I yelled.

We formed a MARATHON MOUSE CHAIN. It worked! We didn't get carried away by the river. Slowly, the waves subsided.

We were ready to race again!

GREAT-GRANDMOTHER STINKYFUR

I was about to take off when I saw a runner by the side of the road. She was staring sadly at the ground. Tears trickled down her fur.

"Are you OK?" I asked.

The rodent wrung her paws. "I've lost my **WATCH**. It means so much to me. It belonged to my great-grandmother Stinkyfur. Oh, I just have to find it," she sobbed.

I felt sorry for her. I felt sorry for Great-Grandmother Stinkyfur, too. I mean, did her fur actually stink? I figured now wasn't the time to ask.

Instead, I searched the ground for the lost watch.

Time passed. The other runners were long gone.

"I don't want to keep you, Mr. Stilton," the mouse said, sighing. "Please go back and finish the race."

At that very moment, I thought I saw something SHINING in the dust. I bent down. Could it be? It was!

"My watch!" the mouse squeaked. She threw her paws around me in a bone-crushing hug.

CHEESEBALLS IN THE ROAD?

I took a deep breath and rejoined the race. I was feeling pretty **STRONG**. I could hardly believe it. I was doing it!

Two seconds later, the muscular rodent in front of me fell to the ground. What was it this time? Cheeseballs in the road?

I looked around. Nothing seemed unusual.

"Are you okay?" I asked the muscular rodent. By now, he was rolling around on the ground, clutching his tummy.

"Oh, I am such a fool!" the mouse cried. "I stopped at that Spicy Rat stand on the side of the road. *Now I have an awful stomachache.*"

I nodded sympathetically. I mean, who can resist a piping-hot cheddar burrito? Yummy!

"Ahem, well, maybe I can help," I offered. "I have a weak stomach, too." I pulled a Swiss–cheese–flavored mint from my pocket. "**HERE, TRY THIS,**" I squeaked.

The big mouse sat down on the curb and popped the mint in his mouth. A few minutes later, he jumped up.

"Geronimo, you're my hero! I feel like a new mouse!" he squeaked. Then he smacked me on the back in thanks and took off.

Forget Bigpaws, that mouse should change his name to *Gigundo* Paws!

I LOST
MY MOMMY!

I was still checking for broken bones when I heard a mouse crying. What now? Had someone twisted a tail? Lost a lottery ticket? Forgotten to cross at the green and not in between? Then I spotted a very small mouse crying behind a bush.

"I LOST MY MOMMY!" he wailed.

I had to stop. What could I do? After all, I am a gentlemouse. I picked up the tyke and dried his tears.

"My name is *Geronimo Stilton*," I told him. "Why don't we go find a nice policemouse? He'll be able to help us look for your mommy."

The little mouse smiled. Then he blew his

nose on my shirt. Oh, the price of being a gentlemouse.

I led the little mouse to the police station. Within a few minutes, a female mouse came rushing in. "Pipsqueak!" she cried. "I was worried sick about you! My glasses fell off, and I couldn't find you in the crowd." She picked up her son and hugged him tight.

Then she hugged me. Then a policemouse. Then a chair, a desk, and a filing cabinet before she headed out the door.

I grinned, and set off on the race again.

Pipsqueak and his mother

THE PRETTIEST BLUE EYES

I was just starting to pick up the pace again when the mouse next to me tripped.

"**Ouch!**" she cried, rubbing her paw. Her name was Sugarsnout Snap, and she had the prettiest blue eyes I had ever seen.

"*I think I sprained my paw! I guess I'm out of the race,*" Sugarsnout said, sighing.

I felt awful. I just had to do something. "Let's go to the first aid station. I'm sure they'll be able to help you," I suggested.

Sugarsnout leaned on my shoulder, and off we went.

It took us a while to get the first aid station. It must have been two thousand miles away. Well, OK, maybe not two thousand, but you get the picture. It took us **forever**!

Lucky for me, Sugarsnout was great company. We talked about books and food. Two of my favorite topics! Yep, that Sugarsnout was a mouse after my own heart.

When we reached the first aid station, I was having so much fun I didn't want to leave. But Sugarsnout told me to go on ahead. She'd meet me at the **finish line**.

Now I had another reason to make it to the end!

JUST LIKE
SUPERMOUSE!

I scampered off again. As I passed the twenty-third mile marker, I saw a mouse who looked just like my dear aunt Sweetfur.

"That's it, young mouse! You can do it!" she shouted encouragingly.

I *smiled* and waved. That's when I noticed a shifty-looking rodent. He was standing right next to the Aunt Sweetfur lookalike. In a flash, he **GRABBED** her pocketbook and ***TOOK OFF*** into the crowd.

Help!

I had to do something! I ran after the thief. My heart POUNDED with fear. What if he had a weapon, like a can of rodent spray? Was I ready to go paws-up for a pocketbook?

I glanced back at the little old lady mouse. She was sobbing into her little-old-lady-mouse handkerchief. I felt a **surge** of energy. With one final lunge, I grabbed the thief's tail. I ripped the bag out of his paws and returned it to the old lady.

"You were just like **SUPERMOUSE**," she sighed.

I wished it were true. I was feeling more like Totally **Exhausted** Mouse.

THE BRIDGE OF SQUEAKS

I stumbled back into the race. At last, I reached an enormouse bridge. I remembered Champ had told me this was called the Bridge of Squeaks. Now I knew why. It was at such a steep angle, it took every last **squeak** to make it across!

All of the runners around me were groaning. I heard one cry, "**THAT'S IT! I'M DONE!**"

Another sobbed, "**I've got too many blisters! I'll never make it to the end!**"

"This is **crazy**!" a third wailed.

I felt the same way. What kind of a nutty mouse wants to run a marathon, anyway?

Just then, I spotted *Old Rat Rickety*

running nearby. He had a huge smile on his face. Speaking of **nutty**! Then I remembered the old rat's words of advice: *Never give up. Never stop believing in yourself.*

I took a deep breath. If Old Rat Rickety could do it, so could I. I scampered forward with every last bit of strength in my paws.

I was almost to the top of the bridge when a terrible thing happened. A runner fainted and fell into the water below!

What could I do? I had to help.

Before I could talk myself out of it, **I dove in after him**.

The water was colder than the super-chilly deep freeze slushy at The Icy Rat ice cream parlor. Even my whiskers were **frozen**. But I didn't have time to think about that. I searched frantically for the runner. Then I saw him sinking below the surface of the water nearby.

CHEESE NIBLETS! He looked just like, well, a drowning rat! There was no time to lose. I dove down under the water and grabbed him by the tail. Then I swam to the surface.

Suddenly, I heard a roaring sound above me. I looked up and saw a helicopter. It was coming to rescue us.

I looked up and saw a
helicopter . . .

"**Here! We're over here!**" I shouted, waving my paw in the air.

The helicopter lowered a long metal cable with a life ring attached to the end of it.

Once I grabbed on to the life ring, the rescue workers pulled me and the other runner up together.

They wrapped us in **warm** blankets. The doctor checked us out. I was fine, but the runner I had saved needed to rest overnight in a hospital. They delivered him to a waiting ambulance.

"Now where can we drop you, Mr. Stilton?" the helicopter pilot asked me. Lots of places came to mind, like a gourmet cheese shop or a tropical island. But a little voice inside my head kept nagging me. It said, *Never give up! Never give up!*

What could I do? I had to go on with the marathon. That voice was giving me a mouse-size **headache**! I asked the pilot to drop me off at the exact place on the bridge where I had stopped running.

PEE-YEW!

I caught up with some of the other marathoners. We ran across the bridge and through the city streets. We passed by a fish market. **Pee-yew**, it stunk! I tried holding my snout and running, but I kept tripping over my paws. Did I mention I'm not the most coordinated mouse on the block?

Just then, I heard a sound behind me. A sardine truck had jumped the curb. Fish spilled out all over the street! The driver stood nearby, wringing his paws.

"Now what am I going to do?" he moaned. "I have to deliver these fish today."

I felt sorry for him. What if he had been delivering *The Rodent's Gazette*? I would want someone to help him. I had to do something, even if the fish were STiNkY. I organized the other runners to help with the cleanup.

When we were finished, the truck driver gave me a hug. It felt nice to do another good deed. Well, except for the stinky, slimy, fishy part.

I waved good-bye to the truck driver and took off running again. As I ran, I peeked at my watch. Holey cheese! It was late. I didn't have far to go, but at this rate, I'D BE RUNNING INTO THE NIGHT. Yikes! Did I mention I'm afraid of the dark?

FELINIUS FEROCIOUSMUS

I was still thinking about running in the dark when I heard a sound. A strange sound.

Well, actually, it was more of a terrifying sound. It sounded like the meowing of a hungry cat! But what would a cat be doing at a marathon for mice? I GULPED. Something told me it wouldn't be part of the cheering section.

With a squeak, I forced myself to turn around. Big mistake.

I found myself snout-to-snout with a **MASSIVE** beast. It had snow-colored fur, blazing yellow eyes, and **RAZOR-SHARP** fangs. Its claws

Felinius ferociousmus

were so huge, they looked like kitchen knives!

I almost fainted. It was the **huge**, hairy feline I had seen in the paper! Yep, the one that had escaped from the Natural Science Mouseum of Nibbles. *Felinius ferociousmus,* otherwise known as Fifi, stared at me with evil, hungry eyes. This was it. I was a dead mouse. "Good-bye, cruel mouse world!" I sobbed as I turned and raced through the streets.

Behind me, I could hear Fifi licking her chops.

I ran *FASTER AND FASTER*. My aches and pains disappeared. My paws felt as LIGHT as feathers. It's amazing what being chased by a cat can do to a mouse. I felt like an Olympic track star!

"Make way! Make way!" I shouted as I ran. "I'm being chased by a cat!"

The other runners jumped aside. I guess no one wanted to be Fifi's dinner. But me? I kept going at **supersonic** speed for what seemed like forever.

I was so worried about Fifi, I didn't even realize I had reached the finish line. I ran right through the tape and kept on going.

Then I spotted the museum workers making their way through the crowd. In an amazing manuver, they captured Fifi in an enormouse net and took her away.

I collapsed in a heap. "I'm alive!" I squeaked weakly. Then I fainted.

My dear nephew Benjamin was standing over me when I woke up. "Uncle, I knew **YOU** were good, but I never imagined that you would come in first!" he shrieked.

"F-first?" I spluttered.

At that moment, the crowd lifted me up and tossed me high into the air.

"Hooray for Geronimo Stilton!" they cheered. "The winner of the Mouse Island Marathon!"

Tears sprang to my eyes. I felt so happy. So proud. So dizzy. Did I mention I'm afraid of heights?

NEVER GIVE UP!

Old Rat Rickety shook my paw. "Well done, Sonny!" he squeaked. "I'm so glad you took my advice. Never give up. Never stop believing in yourself. And never get your tail stuck in a revolving door. Let me tell you, that hurts!"

I was about to ask Rickety more about the door-slamming incident, when the national anthem of Mouse Island began to play. I was so *humbled*. They were playing it in my honor!

After the national anthem, there was a fancy awards ceremony. Everyone was there: my family, Old Rat Rickety, Honey Fur, even Sugarsnout. I got to stand on the block with the number one on it. Then an official-

NATIONAL ANTHEM
OF MOUSE ISLAND

A thousand tails
raised in the air

A thousand voices
squeak with care

Rodents cheer and
heave a sigh

Sweet Mouse Island
will never die!

looking mouse put a shiny medal around my neck. I could hardly believe it. I felt like I was in the middle of a **CRAZY DREAM**. I mean, how else could I have come in first place? I was the least athletic mouse around. I couldn't lift a half-pound weight. I couldn't jump rope. And I was always the last rodent picked for the team.

Just then, I spotted **Champ** in the crowd. "I'd like to thank my family, and especially my friend and trainer Champ Strongpaws for entering me in this **marathon**," I squeaked.

I watched as a tear slid down his snout. I was glad I had made him proud. Maybe now he'd finally tell me where he'd hidden my precious Cheesy Chews.

Marathon in the Rattytrap Jungle?

A few hours later, we boarded the plane back to New Mouse City. Ah, it felt good to go home. I was so tired. I couldn't wait to kick up my paws and RELAX!

That night, I treated myself to a delicious cheesy lasagna dinner. Then I crawled into bed and fell fast asleep. I dreamed I was vacationing at a peaceful island resort.

The next morning, I went into the office early. I had decided that my dream must have been a sign. Yep, I was in desperate need of a little **R&R**. I would take the rest of the week off and relax at my favorite resort and spa, **THE RESTFUL RODENT**.

But first, I needed to tell my staff. "Excuse

me, I have an announcement to make. I am going to be taking a week off . . ." I began.

At that moment, a very muscular rodent burst into the office. Can you guess who it was? Yes, it was Champ Strongpaws.

"Mr. G, you must have ESP!" he cried. "How did you know I just signed you up for another marathon?"

I blinked. "**ANOTHER M-M-M-MARATHON?**" I stammered.

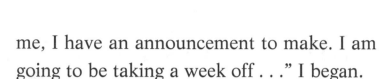

Champ's grin lit up the room. "That's right, Mr. G. You'll be taking part in the RATTYTRAP JUNGLE MARATHON on the Rio Mosquito. Isn't that great?" he cried.

I felt faint. *This isn't happening,* I told myself. The Rattytrap Jungle was the

It's a frightful place, full of snakes . . .

scariest place in the world. I knew, because I'd been there on one of my previous adventures. It was filled with poisonous snakes, raging rivers, and deadly spiders.

No way was I going back there.

But how was I going to tell **Champ**?

I decided honesty was the best policy. After all, that's what my dear aunt Sweetfur always told me. So I calmly explained to Champ that I'm not really much of a SPORTSMOUSE. I like working in my office. I like reading books. I like relaxing in my mouse hole.

Champ just yawned. "Boring!" he snickered. Then he waved an airline ticket under my snout. "Besides, it's too late to back out now. We're leaving in an hour. The marathon is tomorrow!"

My jaw hit the ground. "Tomorrow?" I squeaked.

At that moment, my favorite nephew Benjamin popped into the room.

"Uncle Geronimo, I hear you're going to be in another MARATHON. Can I come with you? Please? Please? I always knew you were like Supermouse," he said.

I agreed. What else could I do? I knew I wasn't like Supermouse, but I really did have a super nephew.

ALL IN ONE DAY

How did it go?

Well, let's just say the JUNGLE is a very, very dangerous place. I was chased by a snapping crocodile, hunted down by a ferocious tiger, and practically strangled by a giant mouse-eating snake. Moldy mozzarella!

Yes, you might even say it was crazier than the **Mouse Island Marathon**. Still, I would always remember my experience in Nibbles. After all, not every mouse gets to run a marathon, nab a thief, save a drowning rodent, survive an earthquake, and catch an escaped *Felinius ferociousmus* all in one day, right?

CHAMP'S
TOP TEN TIPS FOR

BECOMING A
SUPERMOUSE!

1. EAT THE RIGHT FOODS!

Start the day with a good breakfast: It'll give you energy!

Try not to eat too many chips, fried foods, candy, chocolate, or other sweets, when possible. They are difficult to digest and usually don't have the nutrients your body really needs!

Try these, instead. These nutrients will give you lots of energy for exercising.

Fruits and vegetables

Carbohydrates

- *Vitamins and minerals* (fruits and vegetables)
- *Complex carbohydrates* (whole wheat pasta and bread)
- *Proteins* (meat, fish, eggs, beans, milk, and dairy products)
- *Oils* (nuts, fish, cooking oil, and salad dressing)

It's okay to eat all different kinds of food ... but in the right quantities. Not too much, and not too little! To stay healthy, it's important to eat healthy foods and get plenty of exercise.

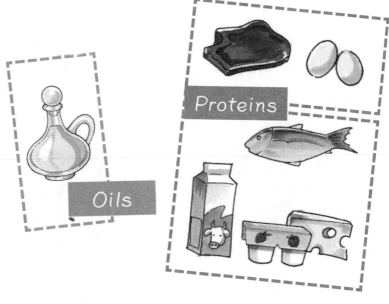

Proteins

Oils

2. DRINK AT LEAST EIGHT GLASSES OF WATER A DAY!

Water is a very important part of staying healthy. Eight glasses is the daily recommended amount.

When you play sports or when it's very hot, you have to drink even more water. Otherwise, you could become **dehydrated.** *Dehydration occurs when you lose more liquids than you actually drink.*

Try not to drink too many fizzy drinks, like soda, because they make your tummy swell up. Drink water, milk, fruit juice, and vegetable juice (which contain the mineral salts you lose when you sweat).

MY TUMMY HURTS!

3. GET EIGHT HOURS OF SLEEP EACH NIGHT!

When you sleep, your cells renew themselves and your body regains the energy you used during the day. Eight hours is a good amount of sleep to aim for. Here is some advice for a good night's sleep:

• Get up and go to bed at the same time each day.

• Don't eat too much in the evening.

• Don't watch too much TV (and avoid scary movies, which could give you nightmares).

No scary movies...

• Before going to sleep, read a few pages of a good book!

• If you're having trouble falling asleep, drink a glass of hot milk (milk contains calcium, which helps you sleep).

...a good book is better!

4. TRY THESE SIMPLE EXERCISES!

Jumping Jacks:

1. Keep your legs together and your arms down at your sides.

2. Jump up a little, spreading your legs and raising your arms. Repeat.

Squats:

1. Keep your legs together and stretch your arms out in front of you.

2. Bend your legs as if you were about to sit down on a stool. Repeat.

1. Keep your legs apart and place your hands on your hips.

2. Lean your body left, then move back to the center.

3. Lean your body right, then move back to the center. Repeat.

Toe Touches:

1. Standing with your legs apart, touch the tip of your left foot with your right hand.

2. Switch and touch the tip of your right foot with your left hand. Repeat.

5. SAY NO TO CIGARETTES, ALCOHOL, AND DRUGS!

Being an athlete also means saying no to cigarettes, alcohol, and drugs.

These things are bad for you! Make the right choices, the intelligent choices. Choose what is best for your body and mind! You'll be healthier and have more energy.

Just Say No!!

If someone offers you cigarettes, alcohol or drugs, talk about it with your parents, teachers, or other adults who you trust. They care about you, and will always give you good advice!

WHEN YOU'RE SCARED . . . USE YOUR HEAD!

Tip number one: If you are feeling nervous before a race, relax. Breathe in and out slowly until you feel calm, strong, and confident.

Tip number two: Before any competition, try to imagine that everything will go well. If you have a downhill skiing race, for example, imagine that you have a great race! All champions do this. And it works. Try it!

Tip number three: If you are still feeling afraid or nervous, remember that at the end of the day, it's only a game!

Ready?

Oh, I'm afraid!

7. A FIT MOUSE NEVER STOPS!

Playing sports is good for the mind and the body!

The ancient Romans said: *Mens sana in corpore sano* (a sound mind in a sound body). Sports help release nervous energy and aggression, help you make new friends, help you be part of a team, make you feel more confident, and help you to realize your goals . . . so they also help you overcome any shyness you might have!

Hooray, hooray, we're a team!

8. BE DISCIPLINED, AND KEEP TRYING!

Remember: It's better to exercise a little and often, rather than exercise hard every once in a while!

I swim for an hour, twice a week!

Ooof! I swim for six hours, once every three months!

9. CHOOSE A SPORT THAT IS RIGHT FOR YOU!

Choose a sport that you like, but ask for advice from your doctor, as well as someone who has more experience than you.

Everybody is different: Some people are suited for swimming, others for tennis, basketball, karate, fencing, football or horseback riding . . .

What's your favorite sport?

RESPECT YOUR OPPONENT!

Whatever sport you practice, remember to respect your opponent! A true champion knows how to win, but he or she also knows how to lose!

As the famouse French scholar Pierre de Coubertin said in 1896 when promoting the new Olympics: "The important thing is not to win, but to compete!"

All sports teach us to know ourselves better. They can even create good feelings between athletes of different nations and races!

Two karate experts bow to each other!

**Want to read my next adventure?
It's sure to be a fur-raising experience!**

THE MYSTERIOUS
CHEESE THIEF

I, Geronimo Stilton, am not a big fan of spooky things. But when Stilton cheese began disappearing during my trip to England, I had to do something! That cheese and I shared the same name, after all. Could I find the mysterious cheese thief, or was I in for a big scare? Putrid cheese puffs, what an adventure!

ABOUT THE AUTHOR

 Born in New Mouse City, Mouse Island, Geronimo Stilton is Rattus Emeritus of Mousomorphic Literature and of Neo-Ratonic Comparative Philosophy. For the past twenty years, he has been running *The Rodent's Gazette,* New Mouse City's most widely read daily newspaper.

Stilton was awarded the Ratitzer Prize for his scoops on *The Curse of the Cheese Pyramid* and *The Search for Sunken Treasure.* He has also received the Andersen 2000 Prize for Personality of the Year. One of his bestsellers won the 2002 eBook Award for world's best ratlings' electronic book. His works have been published all over the globe.

In his spare time, Mr. Stilton collects antique cheese rinds and plays golf. But what he most enjoys is telling stories to his nephew Benjamin.

THE RODENT'S GAZETTE

1. **Main entrance**
2. **Printing presses (where the books and newspaper are printed)**
3. **Accounts department**
4. **Editorial room (where the editors, illustrators, and designers work)**
5. **Geronimo Stilton's office**
6. **Storage space for Geronimo's books**

Map of New Mouse City

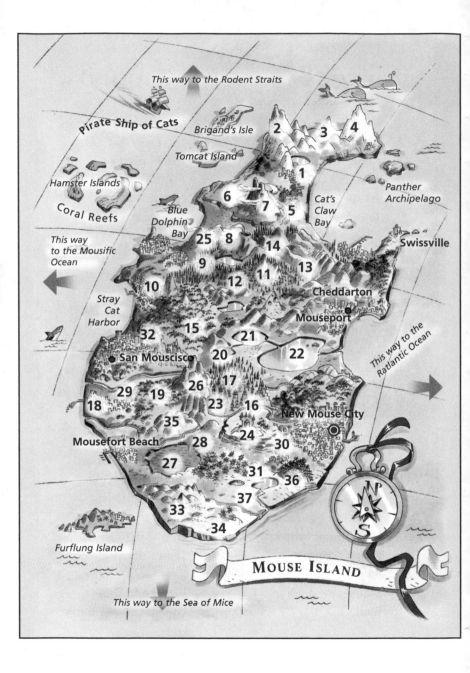

Map of Mouse Island

1. Big Ice Lake
2. Frozen Fur Peak
3. Slipperyslopes Glacier
4. Coldcreeps Peak
5. Ratzikistan
6. Transratania
7. Mount Vamp
8. Roastedrat Volcano
9. Brimstone Lake
10. Poopedcat Pass
11. Stinko Peak
12. Dark Forest
13. Vain Vampires Valley
14. Goose Bumps Gorge
15. The Shadow Line Pass
16. Penny Pincher Castle
17. Nature Reserve Park
18. Las Ratayas Marinas
19. Fossil Forest
20. Lake Lake
21. Lake Lakelake
22. Lake Lakelakelake
23. Cheddar Crag
24. Cannycat Castle
25. Valley of the Giant Sequoia
26. Cheddar Springs
27. Sulfurous Swamp
28. Old Reliable Geyser
29. Vole Vale
30. Ravingrat Ravine
31. Gnat Marshes
32. Munster Highlands
33. Mousehara Desert
34. Oasis of the Sweaty Camel
35. Cabbagehead Hill
36. Rattytrap Jungle
37. Rio Mosquito

Don't miss any of my other fabumouse adventures!

#1 Lost Treasure of the Emerald Eye

#2 The Curse of the Cheese Pyramid

#3 Cat and Mouse in a Haunted House

#4 I'm Too Fond of My Fur!

#5 Four Mice Deep in the Jungle

#6 Paws Off, Cheddarface!

#7 Red Pizzas for a Blue Count

#8 Attack of the Bandit Cats

#9 A Fabumouse Vacation for Geronimo

#10 All Because of a Cup of Coffee

#11 It's Halloween, You 'Fraidy Mouse!

#12 Merry Christmas, Geronimo!

#13 The Phantom of the Subway

#14 The Temple of the Ruby of Fire

#15 The Mona Mousa Code

#16 A Cheese-Colored Camper

#17 Watch Your Whiskers, Stilton!

#18 Shipwreck on the Pirate Islands

#19 My Name Is Stilton, Geronimo Stilton

#20 Surf's Up, Geronimo!

#21 The Wild, Wild West

#22 The Secret of Cacklefur Castle

A Christmas Tale

#23 Valentine's Day Disaster

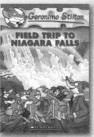

#24 Field Trip to Niagara Falls

#25 The Search for Sunken Treasure

#26 The Mummy with No Name

#27 The Christmas Toy Factory

#28 Wedding Crasher

#29 Down and Out Down Under

and coming soon

#31 The Mysterious Cheese Thief

Dear mouse friends,
Thanks for reading, and farewell
till the next book.
It'll be another whisker-licking-good
adventure, and that's a promise!

Geronimo Stilton